TRICYCLE PRESS
P.O. Box 7123, Berkeley, California 94707
Library of Congress Cataloging-in-Publication Data
Chester, Jonathan
A for Antarctica / Jonathan Chester. p. cm.
ISBN 1-883672-24-4
1. Antarctica—Juvenile literature. [1. Antarctica.] I. Title.
G863.C48 1995 919.8'9—dc20 94-43606 CIP AC
First Tricycle Press printing, 1995
First published in 1994 by Margaret Hamilton Books Pty Ltd
PO Box 28 Hunters Hill NSW 2110 Australia
Typeset in Garamond and Gill Sans by Silver Hammer Graphics
Produced in Hong Kong by Mandarin Offset
1 2 3 4 5 6 — 99 98 97 96 95

A for Antarctica

Jonathan Chester

Tricycle Press
Berkeley, California

Aa

Albatross

These giant sea birds roam the oceans at the bottom of the world.

Aurora Australis

Multi-colored curtains of light often shimmer in the Antarctic night skies. However, they are only visible in winter, as in mid-summer the sky is light around the clock.

Cc

Crevasse

Giant cracks form in the ice when glaciers twist and turn. Deep crevasses are icy blue in colour.

Compass

An ordinary compass becomes inaccurate when used close to the magnetic pole. A sun compass (bottom) is more reliable in Antarctica.

Bb

Boat

Expeditioners often ride from ship to shore in inflatable boats.

Balloon

Balloons are used by meteorologists to study the weather.

Boots

Warm boots must be worn at all times.

Dd

Dog

Some special breeds have a thick double layer of fur and can live out in the snow the whole year round.

Dolphin

The Hourglass Dolphin is the only species of dolphin found in Antarctic waters.

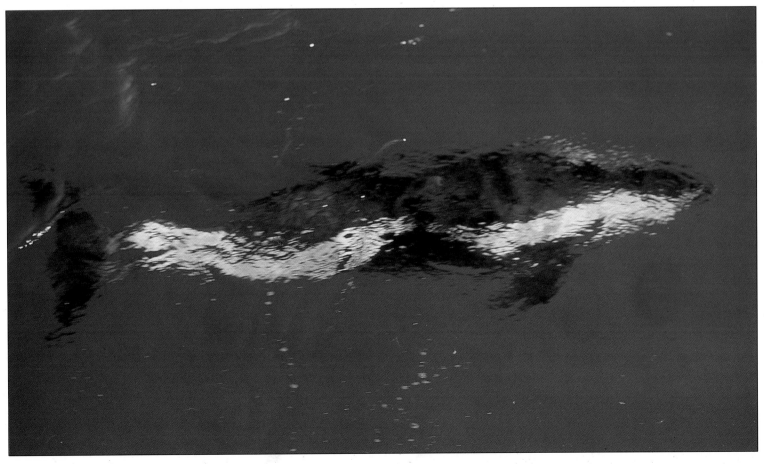

Ee

Explorers

In 1909, less than one hundred years ago, the first party of explorers reached the South Magnetic Pole. In 1988 the first team climbed to the summit of Mount Minto, (4163m) the highest peak in North Victoria Land.

Ff

Fossils
Fossil fish indicate that millions of years ago many parts of Antarctica were under the sea.

Footprints
Climbers leave footprints in the soft snow as they cross a glacier.

Gg

Glacier

Massive rivers of ice flow to the sea. When they begin to break off and float, icebergs are formed.

Greenpeace

This international environmental organization has taken an active role in the preservation of Antarctica as a wilderness.

Hh

Huskies

These powerful snow dogs have pulled sledges across the Antarctic ice for nearly one hundred years.

Hut

The wooden hut built by famous Antarctic explorer Douglas Mawson and his expedition is no longer weatherproof. A nearby modern fibreglass hut provides much more secure shelter.

Ii

Icicles

When the sun melts the snow it sometimes refreezes into beautiful tapers of ice formed by dripping water.

Iceberg

Only a fraction of these floating islands of ice can be seen above the surface of the ocean. Some icebergs are hundreds of meters deep and thousands of square kilometers in area.

Icebreaker

These ships have specially strengthened hulls and very powerful engines. They can break through thick ice and are used to deliver supplies to the scientific bases around the Antarctic.

Jj

Jacket

A warm jacket and hood are essential protection against the freezing cold and icy winds of Antarctica.

Junk

Rubbish left behind by the early explorers (bottom right) is today preserved as historic artifacts. Modern junk, however, is loaded into containers (below) and shipped back to where it came from.

Kk

Krill

These are tiny shrimp-like creatures which live in the sea. They are the main food for most of the fish, birds, seals and even the giant whales in Antarctica.

Ll

Light

A powerful searchlight helps the ship's captain navigate at night through the pack ice.

Mm

Moon Mountains

A beautiful moon rises over the dramatic Transantarctic Mountains, a chain of peaks that stretches all the way across the Antarctic continent.

Moss

These simple plants grow in warmer, moist areas such as the sub-Antarctic islands and on the Antarctic peninsula. Elsewhere in Antarctica it is mostly too cold for mosses to survive.

Nn

Nest

The snow petrel nests in cracks in the rocky outcrops around the coast.

Nunatak

The name the Inuit (Eskimo) gave to a peak of rock projecting above the icecap. Only between two and four percent of the Antarctic is snow free.

Oo

Oasis

In Antarctica this is the name given to regions of low rocky land that are permanently free of snow and ice.

Ocean

The Antarctic continent is completely surrounded by stormy oceans.

P p

Penguins

These flightless swimming birds are found only in the southern hemisphere. Some species, such as the Adelies (opposite top) and the stately Emperors (opposite bottom), are found only in the Antarctic, while others, like the King Penguin (right and below), are found in the sub-Antarctic.

Qq

Quad

Four-wheeled motor bikes (Quads) with their balloon tires have become a popular means of travel around some research stations in Antarctica.

Quest

Even today explorers continue their quest to reach a goal such as the summit of a mountain.

Rr

Radar

Ships' officers use radar to detect icebergs in bad weather or when travelling at night.

Rookery

A colony of nesting penguins lives in a rookery. They incubate their eggs on piles of small stones and each pair defends their territory vigorously.

Ss

Skis
Snow

Skis are used to slide over the snow. They prevent skiers from sinking into the soft snow and minimize the danger of falling down crevasses.

Signpost

Signposts have been erected on many stations in Antarctica to show the vast distances to other parts of the world.

Seals

Most seals spend only the summer months in the Antarctic. The Weddell Seal (top right) is the most friendly, while the Elephant Seal (opposite bottom) is the largest.

Tt

Tent

The traditional polar pyramid tent provides secure shelter for a team of three even during the worst blizzards. A tunnel-like entrance helps keep out the wind and snow. Once made of heavy canvas, today very strong nylon is used in the construction of tents.

Uu

Underwater

Diving underwater in Antarctica is very cold, but marine life is extremely plentiful in the oxygen-rich water.

Underwear

Long underwear is often worn, but normally it is covered by layers of warm clothing. This picture shows the author in his long underwear.

Vv

Vehicle

Tracked vehicles are used to travel over the soft snow. Here a Swedish-made Hagglund crosses a tide crack in the frozen sea ice.

Vest

Filled with down (tiny feathers), a vest is often worn for extra warmth and protection.

Ww

Waterfall

Waterfalls are a rare sight in Antarctica, but occur sometimes in summer, when the sun shines around the clock.

Whale

The largest of the mammals, whales were once plentiful in Antarctic waters, but today the Humpback is seldom seen.

X Marks the Spot

Surveyors use X to mark the spot as a reference point, when mapping in Antarctica. These marks are large so they can be seen on aerial photographs.

Yy

Yacht

Some private expeditions still sail aboard small yachts to reach the southern continent. The Australian Bicentennial Expedition sailed from Hobart to Cape Hallett in this 21m steel-hulled vessel.

Zz

Zero

Water freezes at zero degrees centigrade. The air temperature in Antarctica is below zero most of the time.

Zipper

Survival suits (below) are necessary in the extreme conditions of Antarctica. Zippers make them easy to put on and take off.

Zooplankton

These tiny sea animals can be seen only under a microscope. They provide food for the krill and are a vital link in the Antarctic food chain.

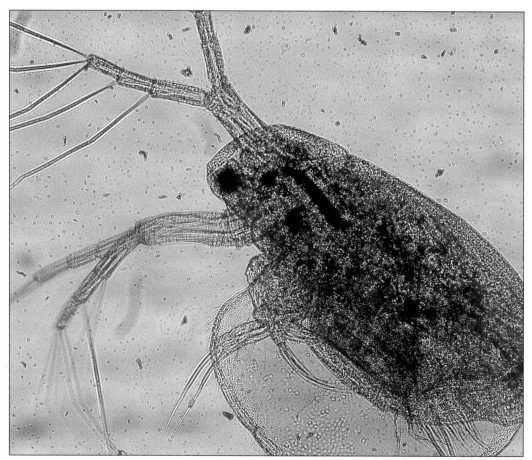